Deception

-A Novel Written by-
Shameek A. Speight

Copyright © 2013 by True Glory Publications

Published by True Glory Publications, LLC
First Edition

Facebook:
https://www.facebook.com/shameek.speight

Instagram: http://instagramcom/bless_45

Email: Shameekspeight199@gmail.com

Twitter: https://twitter.com/Bless_45

Please follow my fan page at
https://www.facebook.com/pages/Sahmeek-Speight

system, without the written permission from the publisher and writer. Because of the dynamic nature of the Internet, any Web addresses or links contained in this book may have changed since publication and may no longer be valid. The views expressed in this work are solely those of the author and do not necessarily reflect the views of the publisher and the publisher hereby disclaims any responsibility for them.

Chapter 1

Patrick sat back in his leather brown lazy boy chair with a letter in one hand and a glass bottle of Jack Daniels in the other hand. "Lord why? Why?" he asked repeatedly as tears streamed down his face. He stared at the words in the letter and couldn't believe what it had said. "NOOO!" he shouted dropping down to his knees and spilling the bottle of whiskey over soaking into the carpet floor. He cried hysterically, "What is my life without a family? What's the point of going on? A real man isn't a man unless he can provide and take care of his loved ones," Patrick mumbled while his salty tears traveled down his cheeks into his mouth. He looked up and could see his chrome revolver 3.8 subnose handgun on the coffee table. He went and grabbed it and sat back down in his lazy boy chair. He opened the revolver barrel and emptied all the bullets out, but one. He spun the barrel of the revolver and placed the gun against his temple. "She loves me!" Patrick said out loud squeezing the trigger while flinching and shutting his eyes at the same time. The clicking sound from the revolver and the fact his head wasn't blown to pieces let him know he wasn't dead. "She loves me not!" he said squeezing the trigger again, only hearing a clicking sound again. Squeezing the trigger a third time, he heard a clicking sound. "Ughh, why Lord just let me die, please?" he shouted. Sounds of the house front door opening caused him to stop crying. He picked up the pieces of paper off the floor, and then stood up. He could see his beautiful wife and his son placing bag after bag of groceries onto the table.

Samantha turned around and could see a deranged look in his eyes. "Why are you crying? What's wrong? Come help me put up all this food," she said in a lovely tone.

"You fucking bitch! You damn hoe! I'll kill you!" Patrick shouted.

Before Samantha could register what was taken place, she was screaming for her life. "AAHHH! AHHH stop!" she yelled as he repeatedly hit her over and over in the face with the gun.

"You bitch! You crazy bitch! I love you!" he shouted and swung with all his might, hitting her so hard that the gun broke to pieces. She collapsed to the hard floor lying there lifeless.

"Nooo! Leave my mom alone, Patrick!" he yelled at him jumping onto his back.

Patrick leaned forward flipping his son forward onto the floor next to his mother and punched him in the face twice. The first blow knocked out his son. "What have I done?" Patrick said with his facial expression twisted up in disgust while looking down at his family. He wiped his tears with his forearm. "This isn't my fault. I'm not to blame for this," he said then walked over to the kitchen sink and opened a drawer, then grabbed the duct tape. He walked back over to his family and duct taped his wife's hands and feet first, then his son. He opened the front door of the house and stared outside from it in a daze as snow fell from the sky covering the ground. He snapped out of the trance he was in and grabbed his wife and son by their legs and slowly dragged their bodies outside. As he pulled them outside through the snow, you could see the impressions left of their bodies on the snow. "It's not my fault! "It's not my fault!" Patrick said repeatedly as he dragged them in to the darkest of the night.

Patrick took another sip from the bottle of Jack Daniels, the only cure for his anger. The snow was falling hard and sleet covered the road making it hard for him to keep control of his GMC Suburban truck from swerving left and right. "Don't you think you should take it a little easy on the bottle, Patrick?" Diego asked while sitting in the passenger seat.

"No! Why the hell should I? The warm whiskey going down my throat is the only thing that numbs the pain. You can have a sip or two if you'd like…. Here," Patrick said pushing the bottle of Jack Daniels in to Diego's chest.

"No, I'm good man. One of us has to have a clear mind. With the way you're driving, we will never reach the top of the mountain," Diego said.

"Well, I'm Irish so you know you can pass the bottle back here," Timothy said.

Patrick turned around and handed Timothy the bottle. He quickly turned his head back around, not to pay attention to the road, but to hide the pain written on his face. If anyone knew him well, it was Diego, Timothy, Murray, Douglas, and Charlie. If he told them what he had planned, they

would have no part of it, but they owed him a favor and it was time to collect.

"Leave it up to Patrick to get us all together to go hunting in a damn snow storm. I don't even know how you got Samantha to agree to you in getting out of the house," Murray said from the back seat.

"Don't you bring up my wife's name. Her name better not come out of your fucking mouth again," Patrick shouted while looking back at Murray causing the truck to swerve all over the road.

"Okay man, okay, just calm down," Murray said while raising both of his hands.

Patrick snatched the bottle of Jack Daniels out of Timothy's hands and took three gulps while driving. It took them seven hours to reach the top of the mountain and then drove through the woods for another half an hour to a cabin. Patrick stumbled out of the truck first and made his way to the nearest tree and pulled out his penis and held it with two hands as it sprayed like a fire hose. His warm yellow pee melted the snow in front of him. He stuffed his penis back in his pants and fought to stand up straight. The whiskey had done its job. It helped him to forget his heartache and the want he had to give up on his life.

Patrick's best friends hopped out of the GMC Suburban truck dressed in all white snow body suits to keep them warm and to help them blend in with the snow for when they were hunting. Murray was African-American of dark skinned complexion and looked like Wesley Snipes twin brother. Douglas was tall and slim built with dark brown hair. Charlie was short and overweight with black hair and green eyes. Timothy was Irish with a long nose and quick to fight anyone, even his friends, but would make up afterwards. Charlie was the youngest of them all. He was outgoing and had a merit haircut. Diego was Spanish and the second in command when they didn't follow Patrick's orders. Patrick was tall with dirty blonde hair and in his early years looked just like Kevin Costner. He grabbed his white hunting rifle out of the back of the truck where they kept other supplies as well. "So, we should go in the cabin and set up, then go straight out. We didn't bring any food like every year we come out here. We eat what we kill and there are a lot of deer out here this year," Douglas said cocking back his rifle.

"I want to start the hunt now," Patrick said through gritted teeth while taking another swig from the bottle of Jack Daniels.

"Why now? We've been on the road for damn near eight hours. I say we eat, then rest up, drink, and share stories," Diego said in a thick Spanish accent.

"I said NO! We hunt now!" Patrick shouted causing all the men to stare at him as if he'd lost his damn mind.

"Okay Patrick, what's really going on?" Murray asked noticing Patrick was acting way out of character.

"You shut up! You don't get to talk," Patrick said while pointing his finger at Murray. He had to use all his strength to continue to stand up straight. "You are my best friend in the world. We grew up together living in the same town, Fort Collins, our whole lives. We hunted on this mountain with our family and served together in the army for ten years together. Never once asking for a favor, but now it's time to collect," Patrick said causing the other five men to become silent as all their minds flashed back and replayed what had took place in Afghanistan.

"Hey, we all promised to never bring that up again, not in this lifetime. What happened over there, stayed over there. Besides, you had a part in it too. You were our Sergeant!" Diego shouted.

"Yes, I allowed it to go down, but we all know I had no part in what took place. Now, it's time for y'all to pay up and have my back as I had each one of yours," Patrick said while taking another gulp of Jack Daniel's whiskey.

"You know we have your back as well. So, what is the favor you need? Just know, that you can only cash in on this favor once," Timothy said while walking over to Patrick. He took the bottle out of his hand and guzzled what was left.

"Damn, I hope you packed more of the good stuff," Timothy said in an Irish accent.

"I sure do. I brought five more bottles," Patrick replied and went to the back of his suburban truck and lifted it up revealing duffle bags and equipment they needed for the weekend. Patrick tossed a few of the duffle bags to the ground. He opened one of the bags and took a fresh bottle of Jack Daniels out of the bag and cracked it open taking a quick sip.

"So, what is this favor that you want, Sergeant?" Charlie asked.

Patrick lifted up a large panel and tossed it in the snow to reveal a secret compartment. Inside the compartment was a brunette haired woman with the skin complexion of ivory, green eye color, high cheekbones, and full thin lips. Her hands and her feet were duct taped together. Next to her was a teenage boy no older than thirteen. He had bright brown eyes that seemed to pull you in. His skin complexion was honey brown and it matched the color of his hair.

"What the fuck!" Diego shouted at the sight of seeing the woman and the boy both tied up in the secret compartment.

"The favor I'm asking all of you to do…. I mean what y'all MUST do, because you owe me, is to hunt my family," Patrick said with a straight face looking all his friends in the eyes.

"What? You can't be serious. That whiskey has finally gotten to you!" Diego said.

"Yes! You know I'll do anything for you, but you're going too far. We came out here to hunt Mountain Lions and Black Bears like we do every year, not to hunt

9

Samantha and Joshua. That's your wife and your son for crying out loud," Douglas stated.

"Hey, I'm in. A deal is a deal. You looked out for me and saved my life. I won't question any order you give me, Sergeant," Timothy stated.

"Hey, I'm with Tim on this one, if you're serious. I'll follow orders," Charlie stated.

"Follow orders? Follow orders? We're not in the damn army anymore. Last time I checked we're all a bunch of grown ass men in our damn 40's and able to make our own decisions. No one's going to stand by while you commit murder or have us apart of it!" Diego shouted and moved toward the back of the truck. He looked down and could see the fear in Samantha and Joshua's eyes. "I don't care if we owe you the world for keeping your mouth shut and turning your head the other way. This isn't right. I will have no part of this bullshit and won't allow you to either," Diego said as he raised his rifle at Patrick's face as he was breathing hard you could see white vapor exit his mouth from it being so cold out. Diego heard the sound of footsteps crushing in the snow. He turned to the side to see Timothy and Charlie creep up on him. "Don't you try it. You both know how good I am with this thing. I'll send a bullet straight through anyone of your heads. Don't test me because both of you know I'll do it," said Diego.

"That's all good and all, Diego, but you'll only be able to take one of us down. After that you'll have a real problem, buddy. By the time you re-cock that rifle, one of us will reach you before the bullet jumps in the chamber and kill your ass," Timothy said in his deep Irish accent.

"Yea, but no one wants to make the first move because no one wants to die. All of you drop your rifles and put your hands up now!" Diego shouted. All five men dropped their rifles to the ground on the cold snow. Diego eased back over to the trunk of the truck and slowly moved his right hand to his waistline and pulled a black folded knife from a holster on his belt, and flicked it open. "Don't worry, Samantha, I'm going to get you and Joshua out of here," Diego said as he cut the duct tape off of her hands, then her feet and then cut the tape off Joshua. He took his eyes off the other five men for a split second and wished that he didn't.

Patrick lifted up his white snow jacket and pulled out a 9mm from a holster on his waistband with the speed of lightning and squeezed the trigger two times. A bullet tore through Diego's left shoulder. "AAAAHHHH," he hollered in excruciating pain and dropped his rifle. The second bullet slammed in to his stomach ripping out of his back and blood squirted everywhere as he fell backwards on to the ground. The white snow turned red as blood poured out of his wounds and on to the snow. "UGGHHH," he groaned and squirmed around in pain on the ground. Patrick grinned and walked over to him. He looked down at Diego and pointed the 9mm at the center of his skull. "I sacrificed for you and you crossed me when it's your turn. Now, you die you disloyal bastard," Patrick said and slowly squeezed the trigger.

"AAAHHH!" Samantha screamed as she hopped out of the secret compartment in the truck and side kicked Patrick causing him to stumble. Before he could regain his balance, she picked up the rifle gripping the barrel of it with both her hands knowing she had no time. It was react or die. She swung the gun upward like a cricket bat. The back of the rifle slammed into Patrick's chin with tremendous force knocking him backwards on his ass.

"Joshua hurry come on!" Samantha shouted. As Joshua hopped out of the secret compartment of the truck, Samantha snatched up one of the duffle bags real fast. With her son by her side, they took off running.

"Wait! Wait! Please, help me!" the sound of Diego speaking weakly stopped her in her tracks. She turned around and helped him off the ground. Diego wrapped his left arm around her shoulder and neck using it as support. They again took off running towards the wooded area. "We'll lose them in the trees," Samantha stated.

Patrick popped up from the ground and ran in the direction towards where Samantha and his son had run. He could still see Samantha and Diego's backs as they moved closer to the woods. Patrick raised his gun and yelled, "AAAAAHHHH!" while squeezing the trigger repeatedly shooting wildly.

"AAAAHHHH…. UUUGGGGHHH!" Diego screamed as one of the bullets slammed into his back.

"What happened? Are you okay?" Samantha asked feeling his body go a little limp as she was carrying more of his body weight.

"I've been hit," Diego moaned.

Tears streamed down Patrick's face, the freezing cold wind did its best to freeze them on to his cheeks which hurt more than the blow he received seconds ago. "I'll get you, Samantha. This isn't over, not by a long shot!" Patrick shouted continuing to squeeze the trigger to his gun hearing a clicking sound only. That let him know the gun was emptied. He pulled out the old clip and put in a fresh clip in. "You can run, Samantha, but I'm coming bitch!" Patrick shouted as he watched them disappear into the woods.

Chapter 2

"What the fuck was that? All of you are well trained and just stood there like deer's caught in headlights. What the fuck was that about?" Patrick shouted at the four men.

"Your ass would have been stuck if one of us brought our family way up to the top of Silver Peak Mountain and tried to kill them. And said, 'Hey fellas, I need y'all to help do it," Murray stated. Patrick just stared at him without saying a word.

"Hey, I didn't know if you were serious or not about this, sergeant," Douglas said breaking the stare down between Murray and Patrick.

"Well now you know I motherfucking am. I kept y'all secret now fucking help me. I will take the blame for this shit. Now, grab your gear and lets go. Samantha now has a head start before us and a duffle bag of supplies, plus a god damn rifle. This will be just like Afghanistan men. The enemy is armed and dangerous," Patrick said.

"Are we really going to do this?" Douglas asked.

"I guess so and without question. He would do it for us!" said Timothy as he strapped on a book bag full of supplies and grabbed his rifle.

Samantha ran as her life depended on it, and it did. She knew her husband would kill her without thinking twice about it. "Mom I'm tired. Why is dad doing this?" Joshua said while stopping in tears. Samantha stopped beside him while still holding Diego. She looked at his once previous white coat starting to turn even redder, and then she stared at her son making eye contact. "I love your brown eyes, my first love, and only child. I can't fail you, and let you die out here. You have your whole life ahead of you," Samantha thought to herself. "Daddy's not himself, baby, but we can't stop running. We must get more distance between them and us before we can rest. Practice your football exercises like running laps. You must keep going, baby," Samantha said.

"But," Joshua started to reply, but was cut short.

"No buts young man. Run and run fast, now!" Samantha shouted and they took off cutting through the woods running in the deep snow that came up to their ankles.

"Stop! I can't go anymore!" Diego shouted.

"Yes you can. You must keep going," said Samantha.

"We've been running over twenty minutes. I'm weak and only slowing you down. At this pace, it won't matter how far we go. They will track us down and kill us," Diego said as he removed his arm from around Samantha's neck and rested his back on a tree. He slowly slid down the trunk of the tree until he was sitting on the ground at rest.

"I just can't leave you. You, me, and my son...we have to keep moving," Samantha replied.

"It's too late for me; I'm nothing, but dead weight." Diego said while removing his snow coat. "Here the blood will dry fast. Have Joshua wear it or he'll freeze to death," Diego stated.

"I'm not fucking leaving you!" Samantha shouted.

"You have no choice. It's stay with me and die or take your son and do your best to get down this mountain and get some damn help. Now, fucking go before it's too late!" Diego said.

"Are you sure about this?" Samantha asked.

"Yes, I'm losing too much blood and they will follow it straight to us. But, I'm going to lead them off in another direction opposite of you," Diego stated.

"Thank you!" Samantha said shaking her head. She looked at her son and passed him the bloody white snow coat and removed the tape from his wrist. She wiped the tears off his face. "I need you to stay strong now. We've got to keep moving okay," she said.

"Yes mom," Joshua said while fighting back his tears. Samantha used the strap to put the rifle on her back, held the duffle bag tightly, and took off running with her son by her side.

"UGGGHHHH," Diego groaned in pain as he eased up off the ground. The freezing wind slowed down his bleeding some, but not completely. He knew it was a matter of time before he bled out like a stuffed pig getting ready to be cooked at a BBQ. He limped towards the east; the opposite direction of Samantha and her son took off running. The more he walked the more he could feel his body get weaker. He looked behind himself to see the thick trail of blood. "It's like I'm leaving bread crumbs for the wicked witch to follow me. I just need to stay alive long enough to buy Samantha some more time. I must keep moving!" Diego thought to himself as he stumbled while walking, each step was harder than the last as his foot sank deeper and deeper in the snow.

"Huh what?" he said out loud as he heard large footsteps not too far behind him. He looked behind him and had to blink his eyes four times. "I must have lost so much blood. I can't believe what the fuck I'm seeing. There stood a Mountain Lion a few feet from him licking up the blood in the snow, but that's not what surprised him at all. He had been hunting on Silver Peak Mountain for years and had seen and killed many Mountain Lions and deer's. His body trembled in fear as the Mountain Lion stopped licking up the blood and stared straight into Diego's eyes. What really made Diego tremble wasn't the fact that he might get eaten alive, but the fact that this Mountain Lion was rare. You could run and hide and still wouldn't see it come. He had to weigh 220 pounds or more. His eyes were bright green with paws the size of two men hands together. All of this was normal to see, but what wasn't normal was the fact that the Mountain Lion's fur was the color white just the same as the snow. As the snowflakes fell down, he blended right in with the snow and it was almost impossible to see, if it wasn't for the red blood around his mouth from just licking and his eyes that seemed to glow. "GRRRRR! GRRRRR!" the Mountain Lion let out a low growling sound.

"Oh shit! Oh shit!" Diego said. His hand shook as he stuck it in his right pocket and pulled out his small folded pocketknife flipping it open. "I'm too fucking weak to run. Besides, I can't out run that shit. My only chance is to put up a fight," Diego said out loud to himself as the Mountain Lion stared at him as if he was a T-bone steak. The Mountain Lion took off running, charging towards him. "Fuck this shit!" Diego shouted from seeing the large cat running at top speed. "Mierda! Mierda!" he screamed shit in Spanish and turned to run. He took only three steps before the mountain lion leapt up in the air. The weight from the huge cat knocked Diego straight to the ground. "AAAAAHHHHH!" Diego hollered in excruciating pain as the mountain lion sunk its long teeth in to the back of his skull. "AAAAHHHHH!" Diego continued to scream and cry the Mountain Lion was biting deeper and shaking Diego's head from side to side in hopes of snapping his neck. Diego swung in an awkward angle backwards and the knife cut the mountain lion on its arm, making the Mountain Lion release its grip. "NOOOOO! Help me!" Diego cried out while crawling away. Then, he felt teeth sink in the back of his calf muscle. "AAAAAHHHHH!" he hollered as the mountain lion ripped away the lower half of his leg and sat down sucking the meat off the bone. Tears streamed down Diego's cheeks, "God, please just let me die before that thing eats me alive. Please just take me Lord." Diego did a push up and flipped himself over off his stomach and on to his back creating a loud smacking sound. He looked at the Mountain Lion eating the lower half of his leg, as if it was an overgrown chicken bone that was baked in the oven for hours, making it nice and tender to the point that the meat was just falling off the bone. "Is he fucking moaning while eating my fucking leg?" Diego said wishing his wounds would kill him long before the mountain lion finished devouring his leg, but he wasn't that lucky.

The Mountain Lion stuck its tongue out and licked the blood off his lips and stuck in its fur around them. He stared at Diego when he finished done with what was left of his foot. He stood half way up ready to pounce then ran. "AAAAAHHHHH!" Diego screamed as the mountain lion ripped open his stomach, swallowing large pieces of Diego's flesh. The Mountain Lion sunk his teeth into Diego's right arm ripping it away. "God, forgive me for my sins!" he shouted as his face was ripped off.

Chapter 3

Joshua stopped running and looked back as the sounds of Diego's screams and the mountain lion's roars could be heard echoing through the whole mountains. "Mom was that Diego?" he asked.

Samantha could see the fear mixed with panic all over her son's face, "Joshua, I don't have time to sugar coat anything for you, baby. The growling sounds you heard came from a Mountain Lion," Samantha replied.

"A lion...a lion.... lions live in Africa or where it's warm. Not in the mountains!" Joshua said with a puzzled look.

"They're just called Mountain Lions. You would know them better as Cougars. They're very powerful giant cats that eat larger animals like deer, rabbits, bears, and us at the moment. If a Mountain Lion has gotten Diego it's even more reason for us to keep moving. Mountain Lions are territorial. So now we have to worry about outsmarting it, your father, and his stupid friends," said Samantha.

"But mommy, why is dad trying to kill us? You never answered me? My father never tried to hurt me or once put his hands on me. Dad encouraged me to be strong and said he loved me. So, what has changed?" asked Joshua.

"Joshua, your father is not the same man. Something is wrong with his mind. He doesn't love you or me at the moment. He only wants to kill us," Samantha stated.

"No, not dad. He's not some psycho crazy killer. Something's wrong? You're not telling me everything mom and I know it," Joshua replied.

"I'm still your mother no matter the situation. Watch how you speak to me and just trust me. We must keep moving, now run," Samantha shouted and they took off once more, running fast down the mountain through the woods.

Pain ran through Patrick's heart as he moved through the woods in a fast pace. "Why? Why'd my life turned up like this, why lord?" Patrick thought to himself as he fought back tears, "Fuck the pain, fuck family, they all will cross you. No one loves you; people just want to use you. Kill them all, then yourself; it's the only way to stop the pain and anger. Just to end this life," Patrick thought to himself as he followed the blood trail with Murray, Douglas, Charlie, and Timothy behind him.

Patrick raised his hands signaling them to stop as the trail of blood increased to larger puddles in the snow. Then he saw what was left of Diego's left leg. Patrick had to fight the urge to vomit; Diego's stomach had been torn out and devoured. The meat on his right thigh was missing; the skin on his face was eaten off, along with the top of his skull. "What the fuck did that to him?" Timothy asked, as he got closer.

"A Mountain Lion," Patrick replied.

"Ain't no god damn Mountain Lion rip him to shreds in a short matter of time. I just can't believe that," Murray stated.

"Well, believe it. It was a very fucking large Mountain Lion, unlike ones we ever hunted before. Now, it has the taste of human flesh. It will hurt us, but from the looks of it it's going after Samantha and Joshua. We got to kill it or get to them first," Patrick stated.

"Why should we track the Mountain Lion if it's only going to do the job for us? Judging from what that Mountain Lion left of Diego's leg and you wanting them dead," Charlie replied.

"Because I want to kill them my fucking self," Patrick shouted as his facial expression twisted up in rage. He was getting ready to say something else until the sound of low moaning caught his attention. All five men turned around and jumped back. "What the fuck?" Murray shouted. Diego was still alive moving around on the ground in excruciating pain and looked like a dead zombie. He raised his right hand, which his thumb, index finger, and pinky had been bitten off. "Fuck you," Diego somehow managed to say while sticking out his middle finger. Patrick raised his rifle, aimed, and squeezed the trigger blowing off what was left of Diego's head in to tiny pieces. The other four men looked on in disgust. "Let go, the hurt has only just begun," Patrick said strapping the rifle across his back and heading deeper into the woods.

Chapter 4

Samantha was breathing hard and her legs felt weak. She put her hands together and blew in them, in hopes of warming them up. The heat from her breath eased the pain in her fingers that felt as if they were frozen stiff. A few snowflakes went down her back giving her chills. "I can't run anymore, mom. I'm too cold," Joshua said.

"I know baby, but we got to keep moving. It's a matter of life and death," Samantha replied as she took her son by his hand and continued to walk. She yanked him back, just as he was going to step three paces ahead of her.

"Mommy what's wrong, why did you pull me back?" he said.

"Just don't take another step," Samantha said and scanned the area really fast. She picked up a long tree branch that was beside her and used it to poke the snow in front of her. SNAP! A loud clamping sound echoed through the woods. As a large metal bear trap with spikes closed like a tiger's mouth on the branch breaking it in half causing Joshua and Samantha to jump back. "We can't go that way we have to go right, and then continue on down the mountain. This whole area is filled with bear traps," Samantha stated.

"Why would there be animal traps here, mom?" And what are you doing?" Joshua asked.

"It's the way lazy people hunt. They place traps in an area. A bear or cougar steps on it and they're stuck waiting until the hunter comes back and kills them, but 99 percent of the time the poor animal bleeds to death because the hunter forgets they left the trap there. I'm taking one of these with us. We never know when it might come in handy," Samantha said while bending down and unhooking the chain that keeps the bear trap locked in one spot on the ground. She unzipped the duffle bag and stuffed the bear trap in. "Let's go," Samantha said while getting up. She grabbed her son by the hand and walked to the right to find a way down the mountain. Joshua collapsed to the ground after walking another mile. "Baby, baby, Joshua!" Samantha shouted and dropped down to her knees.

Joshua was lying on his stomach with his face buried in the white snow. Samantha flipped him over onto his back to see Joshua eyes wide open and breathing hard, each breath he took escaped his mouth and lingered in the air. "Mom I can't walk anymore. I'm too cold, can't breathe, and I can't move.

"You're suffering from hypothermia," Samantha said as she looked up at the sky realizing the sun was going down causing the temperature to drop below 36 degrees Celsius. "Your body is losing heat faster than it can produce it. I'm going to have to do something fast," Samantha said doing her best not to panic, even though her heart was beating hard in her chest. She fought back the tears knowing all she wanted to do was scream as loud as she could. 'Lord save my child, but knowing God gives you the tools you need. It's up to you to be smart enough to use them.' She swiftly gathered branches and sticks grabbing as many as she could carry in her arms. She made her way back to where she'd left Joshua. She dropped the branches and sticks, and then grabbed Joshua by the hood of the snow coat to drag him to a tree and rested him up against it. She dug a small patch in the snow and placed most of the sticks and branches in it. "Mommy, what are you doing?" Joshua said weakly.

"I'm going to start a fire to warm you up," Samantha replied.

"No mom, don't start a fire. I'll be okay. I just need to rest," said Joshua. The more Joshua spoke the weaker his voice sounded. Until he stopped talking before he finished his sentence and closed his eyes, and his head tilted to the side.

"No, get up, get up!" Samantha shouted while shaking him by his shoulders. But he still didn't open his eyes; she pulled her hand way back and slapped him with all her might smacking the fire out of his face. She slapped him so hard her hand was in pain.

"AHHHH! Ouch mom! Why did you do that? What did I do?" Joshua shouted opening his eyes.

"Thank you!" Samantha said exhaling with joy from seeing his eyes open. "Whatever you do don't go to sleep, I need you to stay strong baby and stay awake. Hypothermia causes your organs to stop working because you're freezing. If I don't warm you up eventually your heart and respiratory systems will fail, then death," Samantha said while starring at her son. Just the thought of her child dying made her feel a pain deep down in her soul. She found two small rocks and began to bang them together, the friction from the rocks made sparks jump out of them and onto the sticks. "Damn light, fucking light already!" Samantha said while banging the rocks faster and harder, but the wood still didn't catch fire. "What am I doing wrong?" Samantha asked while crying with tears freezing on her cheeks.

"Mommy maybe you need to dry the wood because it's wet because of the snow," Joshua said in a weak voice while trying to fight to keep his eyes open.

Samantha looked at her son and could see his eyelids were shut and then would reopen fast. "Oh God! Oh God! I'm running out of time. Keep your eyes open baby," Samantha said then unstrapped the snapped rifle from around her back and pulled out a clip that held five bullets as long as her fingers. She placed the head of the bullet in her mouth locking her teeth on it and pulled with all her might. She swiftly poured the black gunpowder onto the wood and spit out the head of the bullet. She did it five more times until she only had one bullet left. She placed it back in the clip of the gun. Her finger felt cramped up as if she had arthritis, but knew it was from the cold. She picked up the two small rocks and banged them together as hard as she could. Sparks from them jumped all over the sticks and branches covered in gunpowder. Whoosh! The fire roared to life! The gunpowder helped the wood to burn even faster. "Thank God! Come put your hands in front of the fire baby. It will warm you up and have you back to normal in no time," Samantha said.

"Yes mother," Joshua said weakly stretching his arms out towards the fire. Already his breathing began to return to normal as his body warmed up. "GRRRRR! GRRRRR!" a loud roar echoed through the woods. That sent chills through both their bodies.

Chapter 5

"Mom, should we put out the fire?" Joshua asked while looking into the darkness of the woods listening for signs of movement.

"No we got to keep the fire going it's the only way we will survive the night until the sun comes back up in the morning. Once it rises we will continue to make our way down the mountain," Samantha replied.

"What about the Mountain Lion? You heard it just like I did. What if it comes for us?" Joshua asked trying his best to hide his fear.

"Don't worry baby, I have one bullet left and mommy is a great shot. I won't miss. Besides, Mountain Lions are scared of fire like most animals in the woods. So, we're safe."

Boom! As soon as the words left her mouth a loud gunshot could be heard sounding like thunder and a huge hole burst open in Joshua's stomach. Blood squirted onto her face. "Mom!" Joshua moaned.

"NOOOOO! NOOOOO! Not my baby, not my baby!" she screamed. She aimed her rifle in the direction that the shot came from. She heard footsteps coming from the left of her, then the right, and then straight-ahead. "UGGGHH!" she turned back around to check on Joshua as he groaned in pain, "Baby, please just hold on," she said with her facial expression twisted up in despair as she fought back tears.

The one second she became distracted was the one second she wished she could take back as Timothy charged towards her. She aimed and squeezed the trigger just as Patrick rushed up on her from the left and hit her in the head with the butt of his rifle causing her to miss Timothy's head and the bullet slamming into his shoulder. "You fucking bitch!" Timothy groaned dropping to his knees in pain as blood skewed out of him.

Samantha's head was throbbing like a terrible migraine. She could feel the veins in her head pulsing and she couldn't recall how long she had been unconscious. The sound of Patrick's voice made her eyes open. She tried to move, but couldn't. Her hands were zip tied behind her back and her ankles were zip tied together making it impossible for her to stand. All she could do was move her neck or inch around. She looked towards the tree that she was only two feet away from and could see Joshua groaning in pain and blood pouring out his stomach. The white snow coat he had on was far from white now and his leg twitched every so often.

"Fuck you! I'm not letting you do this. This is your family and an innocent child. Now, I'm taking Joshua to the hospital and there is nothing that you can do about it. I don't care if you tell what happened in Afghanistan. And I'm not Diego y'all won't drop on me that fast," Murray shouted and punched Patrick so hard he flew sideways. He turned around and squeezed the trigger to his sniper rifle shooting Timothy in his left shoulder.

"Why? Why would you do that? You fucking bloody bastard! I just got done patching up the wound in my right shoulder and you shoot me in the left," Timothy hollered in pain while rolling around on the ground.

Murray quickly punched Charlie in the face knocking him to the ground and kicking the gun out of his hand. He turned to Douglas, "Don't you do it, Douglas. I'll hate to have to kill you," Murray shouted as Douglas raised his rifle and prepared to shoot. "Put the fucking gun down Douglas or I swear I'll kill you where you stand. We don't kill children no matter the debt we owe. This isn't fucking right!" Murray shouted.

"Damn, you're right," Douglas said lowering his gun then dropped it to the ground.

Murray kept his eyes on Timothy, Charlie, and Douglas while he removed the large hunting knife from his holster on his waist. He cautiously bent down and cut the plastic zip tie off Samantha's wrist. "Here you're going to have to cut the ties from your ankles while I keep an eye on these fools," Murray said keeping a close eye on Douglas, Charlie, and Timothy who were still rolling around in the snow on the ground in pain sinking into the white snow.

Murray turned around just as Patrick popped off the ground with an army knife gripped in his right hand about to run towards him with his teeth gritted in anger. Just before Patrick reached him, Patrick stopped dead in his tracks. "You take one more step motherfucker and I'll put a bullet in between your eyes," Murray said meaning every word.

Patrick just grinned showing off his perfect white teeth, "I knew in my heart that you would try to stop me. It's always been you all of this time, my own best friend. I bleed for you, killed to protect you, and kept your secret safe. How could you do what you did to me?" Patrick asked as tears streamed down his cheeks.

Murray hesitated before speaking. He started to say I'm sorry, but then stopped. "I don't know what you're talking about. We are best friends so put the knife down. Don't make me kill you," Murray said with a straight face.

"You already killed me. You took the one thing I loved more than my own life, my family. And I can't believe you're going to stand there with a motherfucking straight face denying it all. You fucking snake! You're the dirtiest kind of person in the world with friends like you. Who needs enemies? I took a bullet for you back in Afghanistan. And this...this is how you repay me?" Patrick shouted.

"It just happened. I'm sorry," Murray said keeping his eyes on Patrick noticing he still hadn't dropped the knife.

The huge all white Mountain Lion could smell the blood in the air. He kept his nose turned up sniffing while walking slow knowing he was closing in on its prey. It was as if a smile spread a crossed the lion's face when he starred at Timothy's back with his blood covered coat as he rolled around in the snow. The Mountain Lion looked past Timothy and could see Samantha on the ground with a knife in her hand trying to cut her own foot free of the zip ties. Then he could see Charlie, Douglas, Murray, and Patrick none of them were paying attention to Timothy. The white Mountain Lion licked its chops and took off running at full speed and was behind Timothy in a matter of seconds. He opened his large mouth and his teeth sunk in between the angle of Timothy's neck and shoulder. Timothy's eyes opened up in horror from the new pain now traveling through his body. "AHHHHHHH! What the bloody fuck!" he hollered in excruciating pain in an Irish accent as the cougar's teeth sunk even deeper inside him.

The sound of Timothy's scream caused all of them to turn their heads in the direction of the noise to see the huge white Mountain Lion that blend with the snow shaking Timothy from side to side like a rag doll. "What the hell is that?" Murray shouted as he aimed his rifle and squeezed the trigger sending a bullet towards the

Mountain Lion and it slammed inches from his paw causing him to look up and stare Murray dead in his eyes. Murray's heart felt as if it stopped or skipped a few beats, and then pounded hard trying to escape his chest. He nervously squeezed the trigger once more. The bullet flew out of the gun and slammed into Timothy's thigh. "AAAAHHHH!" Timothy hollered in agony and pain. Douglas and Charlie snapped out the state of shock and disbelief they were in and grabbed their rifles and aimed at the overgrown lion. It noticed the movement and began to back pedal at a fast pace with his teeth still locked into Timothy's shoulder. "AAAAHHHH...Motherfuckers! Help me! Don't let this shit eat me. Help me! Shit shoot me! Anything's better than getting eaten alive! AAAAAHHHHH! Help!" Timothy screamed at the top of his lungs as the cougar dragged him backwards. He was helpless to put up a fight. "Please! Please let them help me," he prayed out loud.

Douglas and Charlie ran forward while firing their guns, but missed the cougar every time. He was moving too fast dragging Timothy deeper and deeper into the woods away from them. Timothy grabbed at a thin tree with his left hand and held on to it for dear life. "AAAAAHHHH!" he screamed refusing to let it go. He could feel the skin on his left arm pull as the mountain lion tugged harder on his right shoulder and neck. "Help! Bloody fucking help me!" he repeatedly shouted and could see Charlie and Douglas getting closer. So could the Mountain Lion. He became furious that someone was about to disturb his meal. Bullets slammed into the trees past the cougar's head. He released his grip off of Timothy and let out a loud roar that Douglas and Charlie felt travel through their bodies.

The Mountain Lion sunk his teeth into Timothy's left arm that he was using to hold on for dear life. One bite from the lion's mighty jaws severed his left arm ripping it off his body blood squirted out into the cougar's mouth and onto the ground making the white snow red. "AAAAAAHHHHHH!" Timothy hollered. The lion licked his lips and wasted no time to bite into Timothy's calf muscle and used his leg to pull him backwards. "NOOOOOO! NOOOOOO!" Timothy screamed while being dragged into the woods at an incredible speed until he could no longer see Douglas and Charles.

Douglas and Charles ran up trying to follow Timothy's screams, but they were becoming faint by the second. They stopped at the tree he was holding just a minute to see his detached arm and hand still locked on the tree. Murray couldn't believe what had just taken place as he watched in horror. "Ugghh! Ugghh!" he groaned in pain as he felt a long knife ripping through his flesh, piercing his rib cage traveling to his lung.

"You lying motherfucker," Patrick said through gritted teeth while stabbing Murray repeatedly in the back left side of his body. Murray dropped to his knees and the rifle fell out of his hand. He coughed up blood and finally fell face first to the ground. Patrick continued his attack. "You stupid ass, how does it feel to be backstabbed? How does it feel? Huh! Do you love it? To know that your best friend is putting the knife in your back," Patrick shouted raising the hunting knife real high and coming down into the center of Murray's back with full force. Murray's body bucked from the force and pain, "Ahhhhhhhhhhh," Murray screamed as Patrick twisted the knife while it was jammed deep inside him. "The pain that you're feeling now is in no comparison to what I feel and how my heart hurts,"

Patrick said then spit on the back of Murray's head.

Patrick turned around and walked back over to the tree his son was resting on. Joshua sat there holding his stomach fighting to stay awake. The bullet had torn a hole in his stomach and a big hole out from his back. Blood poured out of him fast. Joshua stretched out his bloody hand, "Father, help me," he mumbled as tears streamed down his cheeks. In his mind, he couldn't come to grips as to why his father, the man who took care of him, taught him how to walk, how to catch a football, and to carry himself with respect, be causing him so much pain. Patrick's facial expression twisted up in despair as tears flowed out of his eyes like a river. He lifted up his white snow jacket and pulled out a 9mm handgun from his waistline. He aimed at Joshua's heart. His head shook and the water from his eyes from crying made it almost impossible for him to see clear. "Dad why? Why are you doing this? I love you! Don't hurt me no more, please? Please don't hurt me. I don't understand what I've done wrong. Why?" Joshua screamed.

"You were born!" Patrick replied and squeezed the trigger once. The bullet slammed into Joshua's chest and ripped a huge hole into his heart. Joshua's body shook and he dropped an outstretched hand. "Why daddy? Why are you hurting me?" he mumbled.

Patrick raised the gun a little higher and replied, "Blame your mother," while squeezing the trigger sending a bullet crashing right into the middle of Joshua's head splitting it in half. Patrick dropped to his knees and buried his face in the palm of his hands and cried like a newborn baby.

"Noooooooo!" Samantha had watched everything while trying to cut herself from the zip tie from her ankles. Her stomach cramped up and ached. Her heart felt a pain it had never felt before. She broke free of the plastic zip tie. She popped up off the ground picking up a large rock and ran over to where Patrick was kneeled down crying. She swung with all her might knocking Patrick in the head with the rock. You killed our son she shouted repeatedly. The blow was so hard and caught Patrick off guard because he flew sideways and rolled three times making the gun fall out of his hand. Samantha looked at her only child lying there dead with his head split wide open. She screamed at the top of her lungs and couldn't stop the tears from falling. She looked down and noticed the handgun that Patrick dropped and quickly snatched it up. She aimed at Patrick who was rubbing his head as blood leaked out of it. From the corner of his eye, he could see Samantha about to pull the trigger. He scooped up a handful of snow and tossed it real fast. The snowball smashed into her nose and eyes making it impossible for her to see. Patrick rolled as the bullet slammed into the ground into the spot he was just in. Samantha listened to the sound of his movement and continued to fire wildly. Patrick hopped off the ground and took off running for dear life. Samantha wiped the snow away from her eyes and could see Patrick running low at top, stop towards the wooded area. "Ahhhhh!" she hollered and squeezed the trigger repeatedly.

Patrick leaped up in the air and jumped behind some bushes, then ducked fast behind a thick tree. He stuck his head out from behind the tree; pieces of the bark went into his mouth. He spit them out and ducked back behind the tree as Samantha came charging towards his direction while screaming, "Ahhhhhhhhh!" squeezing the trigger of the gun sending a spray of bullets wildly towards Patrick.

"Oh shit! Oh shit fucking crazy bitch!" he shouted.

"You killed our son! You killed our son!" Samantha screamed.

"Fuck you bitch! I killed your son, not mine," Patrick shouted back doing his best to act as if he felt no remorse, but his heart hurt. He never knew pain as he felt today.

Samantha felt herself being tossed to the ground as a loud gunshot could be heard echoing through the air. Samantha looked up off the ground to see Murray standing there with over twenty knife wounds in his back and chest. His white snow coat was dripping red onto the snow. He looked down at his stomach to the newly fresh hole that ended his stomach and came out of his back. "Run, run!" he mumbled while coughing up blood just as another bullet slammed into his chest. The impact was so hard that it lifted him off his feet. He landed onto his back groaning in pain.

"I got his ass," Charlie said with a huge smile on his face as him and Douglas ran for cover behind the same tree as Patrick.

"Nooooo! You bastard," Samantha

shouted while continuing to fire in their direction and crawled over to Murray.

"You have to run," Murray mumbled as blood leaked out of him.

"Not without you," Samantha helped Murray up while still squeezing the trigger. She looked at her son one last time and took off running.

Chapter 6

"This is going way too far men. We lost Timothy and killed Diego. And if Murray's not dead, he's not far from it. You shot your own son. I just want out of this blood bath right now," Douglas stated.

"Fuck! Timothy is not dead. I can still hear him screaming. It's faint, but I can still hear it. All we got to do is follow the blood trail and it will lead us to him and that white man eating fucking Mountain Lion!" Charlie stated.

"No Douglas, you can't piss out now! We're in this till the end. Like I said at the end of all this, I'll make sure the police will blame everything on me. I just can't do this on my own. So stop acting like a bitch after all that I have done for you. As far as Timothy goes, he's a done deal. Charlie we can't save him. By the time we'd reach him, it would be too late anyway," Patrick stated.

"How the hell can you say that? We can still save Timothy," Charlie replied.

"Listen, the man's arm was completely ripped off. He will bleed to death. It's just a matter of time. If we go after him now, we'd reach him just in time to see the lion finish him off. Besides if we don't stay on Samantha's trail, we will lose her out here. She was a Marine for five years. She's not as helpless as she looks," Patrick stated.

"I don't like it. We never left a man behind, but lets finish here. So I can hunt the white fucking lion and hang him on the wall," Charlie replied.

"Ahhhhhhhhh!" Timothy's voice became soft and weak from screaming as the cougar continued to drag him deeper into the woods by his leg. "Please guys fucking come! I don't want to die like this. All they have to do is follow the blood smeared all in the snow and shoot this overgrown cat in the head," Timothy thought to himself, as he looked at all the blood that was pouring out the whole where his left arm used to be. He could no longer feel the pain because the freezing cold had numbed some of his nervous system. He felt himself stop being dragged. "Please help!" he screamed in a weak voice in the direction he was taken from as a tear traveled down his cheek onto the snow.

He felt his body flip over suddenly. He was now on his back and his lips trembled in fear as he stared at the large Mountain Lion's head as they now were face to face. The Mountain Lion's mouth was covered in thick red blood mixed with saliva. He opened his mouth wide. Timothy could see nothing but razor sharp teeth the size of fingers. "Ahhhhhhhhh!" he hollered, as his stomach was ripped open. He could feel the Mountain Lion tugging and ripping at his flesh swallowing pieces of him in one gulp. "Nooooo! No this can't be happening!" Timothy cried out as he pounded weakly at the Mountain Lion's face in hopes of getting him to stop. The Mountain Lion grinned with a mouth filled of what was left of Timothy's insides. He sucked it up like linguine pasta then bit off Timothy's right hand and forearm. He chewed four times before swallowing. "Ahhhhhhh! You bastards! You bastards! You could have saved me!" he shouted at the top of his lungs as the Mountain Lion opened his mouth and ate half of his face off. Timothy's body went into convulsions then bucked. His body stopped moving after a few seconds after his body went through shock.

Douglas, Charlie, and Patrick held their heads down in shame doing their best to pretend they didn't hear Timothy's final screams and calling them bastards when they knew in their hearts there was more than enough time to save him. Patrick quickly brushed the guilty feeling off. He dug around in his pocket and pulled out a small bottle of Jack Daniels. He opened it and took three sips. "Let's go before we lose her trail. The sooner we kill the bitch, the faster we can kill that Mountain Lion," Patrick said as he grabbed his rifle off the ground and looked back at his son one last time. He looked at the trail of blood Murray had left behind and took off running with Douglas and Charlie behind him.

"I can't go on anymore," Murray said while breathing shallow and coughing up blood. He dropped to his knees.

Samantha looked at him and knew he wasn't going to make it. She knew it's only been pure adrenaline for the only reason he was still alive now. She dropped down to her knees next to him. His body had gotten so weak. He lay backwards resting his head on her lap. "I'm sorry I let it get this far. We should have killed him months ago, but I couldn't. He's my best friend," Murray said in a weak voice.

"We should have stuck to my plan and killed him baby. Look what he has done, just look at what he has done. He killed our baby. If I knew it was you he had in the back of the truck, I would have stopped it before it had gotten this far. But, how did Patrick find out about our son?" Murray said as blood leaked out his body fast like a Capri sun juice box with over fifty holes in it.

"He found the letter," Samantha said while crying and rubbing his head. She knew it was only a matter of seconds before he was gone forever.

"What letter?" Murray asked with a mix of confused with painful look on his face.

"I took a DNA test on Joshua and sent it out. I couldn't really go through the plan of killing him until I was sure Patrick was the father or not."

"So, I guess I was the father, huh? Samantha, when you first came to me and asked me to help you conceive a child I thought you were out of your mind. I always wanted you, but couldn't betray my best friend like that. You came to me asking every day. I knew it was wrong, but I gave in. From the moment I entered inside you, I fell in love and knew I would never stop. The time you stop when Joshua was born broke my heart," Murray said while spitting out more blood.

"I had to I was married. What we were doing was wrong, but felt so right. But, I needed to be a good wife. I loved Patrick and I loved you at the same time. I honestly thought Joshua was his son at first, but by the time Joshua turned two I knew in my heart, he wasn't. But, I couldn't tell Patrick that. He loved Joshua. How could I tell you he was your son when you loved me? How could I break apart a childhood friendship that's been going on for more than thirty years? I couldn't. But, the more I've been with you, the more my heart became yours. Every time I lied and said I was going to the store just to get away from Patrick, I did just to have you inside me for a half an hour and it was everything to me. We've been lovers off and on for over thirteen years. Now, it was finally time to put the secrets to an end, but the only way we could truly be together was to kill Patrick. I'm so sorry for letting you down baby. I'm so sorry for letting our son down," Samantha said while crying hysterically.

"It's not your fault. We're getting what we all deserve. That man loved us unconditionally and was always there for his friends and family. He would never tell a person no. If it were in his power to help someone, he would do it. We created this monster. We lied to him in the eye. We can't even be mad at the outcome that's happening. This is God's plan or the Devil's game. Anyway, I love and we deserve to die," Murray mumbled then coughed up a mouth full of blood as he made his last and final breath.

"Noooooo! Baby nooooo! Don't go! Don't leave me, please!" she said while tears continued to stream down her cheeks. She bent over and kissed him passionately on the lips and could taste the blood in his mouth. She fought back tears and the pain she felt. "I'm sorry baby, but none of us deserve to die today but Patrick," Samantha said through gritted teeth. She looked up at the grey sky just as four snowflakes fell on her face. She eased Murray's head off of her lap and picked up the 9mm handgun off the ground. She pulled out the clip to see she only had one bullet left. She pressed the 9mm in her jeans on her waistline and pulled the hunting knife out from it that Murray had given her to cut the plastic zip ties off her wrist and ankles.

"I will not die today!" Samantha shouted. She took off running into the woods grabbing long tree branches and bringing them back behind the tree Murray's body rested. She ran at full speed to the area that was covered with bear traps that had snow over them. She stabbed one pulling the pin out of it and carefully closing it. Then she carried it back to the tree. "I swear I will get revenge for those fuckers killing my baby and murdering the love of my life. I'll fucking piss on their faces," Samantha said while using the hunting knife to sharpen the long branches into spears, making the tips of them pointed. She tested the weight and balance of one, took a few steps back, aimed at the tree, and threw the spear with all her might. The speed cut through the air like a razor blade cutting through a thin piece of paper, and slammed into the tree getting stuck deep inside.

A wicked smile spread across her face as she walked towards the tree. She tried to pull her spear out, but it was jammed in too deeply. So she broke it in half. "They will pay for taking my son and my love from me I swear," Samantha said while scooping up most of the spears she made into her arms and placed them in different spots.

Flashbacks of Murray kissing her and him being deep inside her as she lay flat on her back on his kitchen table were going through her mind. "Ahhhhhhh!" she moaned as his long chocolate dick went deep inside her. She spread her legs wide as he slammed his body into hers. "Ahhhhh! Fuck! Yes, yes take this pussy baby. It's yours!" She moaned as her pussy got wetter with each stroke.

"He don't fuck like this, do he?" Murray said while grinding his hips making his dick touch the sensitive walls inside her pussy.

"Ahhhhh! No...no! He don't fuck me like you do baby! My pussy miss this dick all the time," Samantha replied with lust in her voice while staring at Murray's slim, but perfectly built body. The army had done him justice and kept him in top shape. His cinnamon light brown skin complexion turned her on even more. He was the only African American man she had been with. Her body screamed everything she was doing was wrong, that just made her cum even harder. Murray pulled his seven-inch dick out of her soaking wet pussy. He looked at the black digital watch on his wrist and knew he only had another ten minutes with her before Patrick would be concerned with where she was. Murray flipped her around onto her stomach and spread her ass cheeks and worked the heck out of his dick inside her. "I don't care anymore you need to be all mines. We can run away. Fuck this town. Fuck our friends. It's just you and me. This dick not worth leaving everything behind, huh?" Murray said while stroking deep inside her, each thrust felt better than the last.

"Yes! Yes baby! I need this dick all the time!" Samantha shouted as she climaxed. Thick clear cum was running out of her pussy onto his dick and down his thigh. Murray grabbed her by her shoulders to get deeper penetration.

"Uggghhhh!" he groaned while slamming his body into her releasing all inside her, "I love you," he mumbled as he collapsed onto the back of her out of breath.

Samantha snapped out of her daydream and back to reality. "I love you too," she said out loud.

Chapter 7

Samantha could hear the sound of footsteps and knew it was time to go. Patrick, Douglas, and Charlie approached Murray's body lying next to a tall thick pine tree. They kept the rifle high scanning the woods for any movement, and then they finally relaxed when they stood in front of Murray's body. "You know I never question an order and you did so much for me, but only a fool wouldn't ask questions. I got to ask why? Why did you kill your son and Murray? And why do you want Samantha dead so bad?" Charlie asked.

"Because they all broke my heart. Murray was having an affair with my wife for years and I was just too blind to see it," Patrick said while fighting back tears, and then noticed that Charlie and Douglas held their heads down. "Wait! Wait! Y'all knew and never said anything?" Patrick asked dumbfounded.

"Umm...everyone in the town knew, Patrick," Douglas replied.

"So, you both knew this whole fucking time and no one said anything! Why? How could you?" Patrick shouted not believing what he just heard with his own ears. His heart knew so much pain in less than twenty-four hours.

"Patrick, you are the kindest guy in the town and person anyone has ever met. No one had the heart to tell you what we already knew been going on? For crying out loud, Joshua looked like a mixed child, but you told everyone it's because you have Indian in your family. Murray and Samantha had been sleeping together for years. It was none of our business to get involved in that. Besides if we did tell you, this right here would have been the reaction," Douglas replied.

"Ahhhh!" Patrick screamed while looking up in the sky. He took a few steps back to hide his tears from his friends. "Why God? Why?" Patrick shouted. He squinted his eyes as he noticed something way up in the pine tree where Murray's body was lying next to at the bottom. He couldn't make out what he was staring at. Charlie and Douglas looked up to see what caught Patrick's attention.

Samantha sat comfortably on the branch way up in the pine tree. A wicked smile spread a crossed her face as she aimed carefully, then releasing the bear trap. It fell at incredible speed. Before Charlie could realize what the object was, it was too late! The bear trap landed on top of his head and the large metal teeth clamped onto his neck. "Ahhhhhh!" Douglas and Patrick screamed out of shock.

Charlie gasped for air and spit up blood. He dropped his gun and panicked while trying to get the trap off of his head. The large metal teeth were deeply jammed into his neck all around making it impossible for him to scream or speak. He walked in a circle while trying to remove it, but wasn't strong enough. "Fuck! Oh shit!" Patrick shouted as he and Douglas rushed to Charlie's aid. Patrick grabbed one side of the bear trap and Douglas grabbed the neck. "Okay on three we pull together," Patrick said, "1-2-3," Douglas and Patrick groaned while using all their might to pull the bear trap open and tossed it off Charlie's neck. They weren't prepared for what happened next as it caused them both to scream like two high school girls scared of the boogeyman. "Ahhhhhhhhhhhh! Ahhhhhhhhh!" The metal teeth in the trap cut through Charlie's neck so deep that it chopped half of it off. His head now hung sideways only connected to his body by a thin piece of skin. Blood squirted up like a volcano. Patrick and Douglas looked on in horror, as Charlie's body was still moving around walking in circles. His lips moved and Patrick could read them. He repeatedly said, "Help me! Help me!" Charlie grabbed his head and pushed it straight back up onto his neck. His leg buckled as his body became weaker and weaker from the amount of blood he lost. Patrick and Douglas looked on in amazement shocked that Charlie was still alive. Then they heard what sounded like a cry, "Ahhhhhhh!" a scream that had hurt, pain, and anger all in one. They looked up to see Samantha jumping out of the high pine tree with a hand made spear that was six feet long using all her body weight sending the spear through Charlie's open wound. Just as his neck fell to the side once more, the spear traveled through his body and came out between his legs pinning him to the ground. "What the fuck? What the fuck?" Patrick shouted repeatedly. Charlie's head was hanging to the side while his arms and feet were moving, but he was pinned in one spot looking like a human twizzler. "I'm going to kill that bitch!" Patrick shouted while looking as Samantha who had landed behind Charlie.

She was covered in blood with an evil twisted smile. Patrick aimed and fired. Samantha rolled and ducked behind a tree. "You killed our son!" Samantha shouted.

"No woman! I killed yours and Murray's son! How dare you have a love child and I raised him as mine. You have no idea how you destroyed me inside!" Patrick shouted.

"Hahahaha!" Samantha's laughter echoed through the woods, "You deserved it. You were too weak and too fucking kind. You think a woman wants that all the time. A woman needs to be choked and put in her place from time to time. Never once have you put me in my place. You let me walk all over you. You're too nice and too fucking weak. You always make love to me when I needed to be fucked, Patrick. That's what Murray did. He treated me like his little slut. He fucked me hard. He gave me what I needed to carry on another day. Your soft as motherfucker!" Samantha shouted.

"Why are you standing there letting her say those things? Let's kill this bitch," Douglas said looking at Patrick, who had the facial expression of a man, whom had his heart ripped out. He held his head down in shame. "Well, you can stand there and feel sorry for yourself, but I'm not. You're too good of a friend and person for this shit. I'll kill this bitch myself!" Doulas shouted and took off running in the direction he seen Samantha go.

"Wait! No don't go! Things have changed!" Patrick shouted, but Douglas had already disappeared in the woods. Patrick pulled out the small bottle of Jack Daniels from his pocket and took three sips of it. The warm liquid traveled through his body easing his nerves and heart. "Things have changed were no longer hunting her. She's now hunting us," Patrick mumbled while taking another sip of Jack Daniels.

Chapter 8

   To be a heavy set guy, Douglas was
light on his feet and moved through the thick
snow with ease. Snowflakes falling down
made it almost impossible to see Samantha's
size six footprints in the snow. "I have to
hurry up and catch up to her before the snow
covers her trail. How can a woman or
person be so damn cruel and cold hearted?
I'm going to enjoy seeing that bitch's head
explode," Douglas said out loud to himself.
A smile spread across his face as he caught a
glimpse of Samantha back, she was hopping
through the snow. He raised his rifle and
aimed and squeezed the trigger just as
Samantha ducked behind a tree. The bullet
flew past her head. "Too slow fat boy!
Come get me!" Samantha shouted.
   "Let's see how secretive your ass will
be when I put a bullet in your head! You
broke the heart of the kindness man there is.
You're truly a cold-hearted bitch," Douglas
said while slowly stepping closer to the tree
she was behind. He licked his lips knowing
she was only a few feet away. Even if she
ran out from behind the tree, she had
nowhere to go. "I'll be on your ass like
white on rice," Douglas said out loud then

saw Samantha take off like rabbit hopping over snow and behind a tree a few feet on her right. Douglas squeezed the trigger and a bullet slammed into the snow.

"You're going to have to move faster than that fat boy," Samantha said in a teasing tone.

"Fucking bitch," Douglas replied and stormed off running in her direction. "Ahhhhhhhh!" he screamed at the top of his lungs as he heard a clapping sound. He looked down to see that he had stepped in a bear trap that was covered in the snow making it hard for him to see. The metal teeth of the bear trap were deeply clamped into his calf muscle. "Ahhhhhhh!" he continued to holler in pain. Douglas dropped his rifle and bent over grabbing the large bear trap with both hands to pry it open. The sound of something cutting through the wind caused him to look up. His eyes opened up as wide as a quarter as he seen a spear flying towards him at incredible speed. The spear slammed into his left shoulder ripping through his body. Half the point of the spear now hung out his back. "Ahhhhhh! You fucking bitch. You slut ass hoe!" Before he could finish his next sentence Samantha grabbed another spear from behind the tree and looked like a champion Olympic spear thrower as she sent the spear crashing into his stomach. It ripped through the fat meat of his gut and traveled all the way through. "Ahhhhhhhh! Uggghhhh!" Douglas hollered as his intestines now hung out of his stomach. Another spear flew into the meat of his thigh causing him to fall sideways. His left hand touched the ground covered in the cold snow "Ahhhhh! You bitch!" he shouted as a bear trap went off on his hand sinking its teeth into his forearm. "Ahhhhhh!" he cried out in excruciating pain. He tried to pull his arm free while keeping his eyes on Samantha who had a six-foot spear in her hand and was walking towards him. Fear and pain traveled through Douglas's body. "No... No! I won't die like this," he said as he looked at his rifle knowing he couldn't grab it without his left arm. He knew with just one free hand he wouldn't have the strength to free himself so he pulled with all his might. "Ahhhhhhh!" he hollered in agonizing pain as his skin stretched and tore. He continued to pull even though he wanted to pass out from the pain. He looked on and hollered as his arm ripped in half. "Ahhhhhhhh!" he screamed as he stared at his open wound where his forearm should be. There was now broken bone, raw flesh and meat, and blood squirting everywhere up into his face. He looked down and could see his detached arm still stuck in the bear trap.

"You bastard! You killed my son. Now, I'm going to make every last one of you pay," Douglas heard Samantha's voice say and it broke the trance he was in. Samantha kicked the rifle a few inches away out of his reach and stood behind him.

Douglas had limited movement and was unable to turn fully around, "Please don't! What are you doing? Please don't hurt me no more. I didn't kill Joshua. It wasn't me," Douglas shouted in a terrifying tone as fear consumed his body and his heart raced. He could feel Samantha's size six boot press against the back of his head. She applied pressure pushing him face forward towards the ground. "Wait! Wait! What are you doing? Please stop! I didn't kill Joshua!" Douglas shouted then vomited out of fear. His lunch mixed with everything else he had eaten rushed out of him. The warm vomit landed on a pile of snow in front of his face. The hot fluid from his body melted the snow in front of him. "Ahhhhhhh! Ahhhhhhhh!" Douglas began to holler at the top of his lungs like an old lady being robbed for her purse. "Ahhhhhhh!" With the snow now melted away, he could see that his head was now between a bear trap and his face was only inches away from setting off the pressure pad to make it slam shut closed. The slightest touch will trigger it off. "Ahhhhhh!" he screamed while using his right hand to do a pushup to keep his head leveled. "Noo! Please stop! Don't do it!" Douglas begged.

"Fuck you all! Y'all killed my baby!" Samantha shouted. She raised her foot high and stomped on the back of his head and pulled her leg back with lightning speed.

Patrick stumbled through the woods. "Damn that whiskey is stronger than I thought," he said out loud then could hear Douglas screaming for dear life. He ran towards the noise as fast as he could through the thick snow. He reached the area where the screams were coming from. He looked down and could see a lump in the snow and years of hunting experience kicked in. He stepped over it knowing it was a bear trap. He could see Samantha's back and Douglas on the ground with blood covering the snow. His right leg was stuck in a bear trap, his left arm was ripped off, and the detached hand

and forearm was stuck in a bear trap. Samantha had her foot rested on the back of his head.

Patrick raised his gun and closed his left eye while looking through the scope. He adjusted his aim to the back of her head. "I loved you so much," he mumbled as he fought back his tears and tried to find the strength to kill the second person in this world he loved more than himself. What he saw next broke his concentration. As Samantha stomped on the back of Douglas's head, his forehead touched the pressure plate making it snap close chopping half of his face off. His body bucked and flapped around wildly then stopped as blood poured out of what used to be his face. "Nooo! You bitch!" Samantha turned around and could see Patrick as he screamed. She pulled a spear out of Douglas's body and tossed it. Patrick couldn't make out what the object was until it was too late. The falling snow made it hard for him to see. "Uggghhhh!" the spear pierced his thigh and jammed into it as he groaned in pain. Samantha rolled onto the floor in one swift move and picked up Douglas's rifle while on one knee and she aimed at. Patrick looked up and quickly pulled the spear out of his thigh and took off running, zigzagging through trees.

"Oh you won't get away that easy. I guess the Marines trained me better than you, huh? You motherfucker!" she shouted with a wicked smile on her face. She took off running after him.

Chapter 9

"God maybe I deserve to die. I killed my own son, even if he wasn't biologically mine. He still was my son and I raised him. I taught him how to walk and throw a football. Did I really let this pain, this grief, blind my own judgement to the point I killed my best friend and the people I love? Maybe I should die. No not yet, she has to pay. She was the one wrong, not me," Patrick said to himself while crying. "Uggghhhh!" he screamed as a bullet ripped the side of his face.

"Damn, just an inch closer and I would have hit him in the temple, soft weak ass bastard," Samantha said through clenched teeth.

Patrick rubbed at the new flesh bleeding scar on his face. "I got to get the hell out of here. She will kill me before I even get a chance to get off a shot," Patrick said and ran knowing his life depended on it. He cut through some trees and knew he wouldn't get a far lead ahead of her. He was in his mid 40's and in great shape, but Samantha was in her mid 30's and ran five miles every morning just for fun. "Okay, I can't out run her. Think! Think! Patrick fucking think!"

He spotted two logs and flashbacked to when him and Joshua were riding logs or anything they got their hands on down the hills of snow. He quickly pushed the thought out of his mind, then ran towards the log and hopped on it. He could hear Samantha's footsteps gaining on his position. He turned the log straight and used his legs to get a push start. The slight of snow along with his body weight caused him to slide down the long mountain picking up speed rapidly. He leaned left to avoid a tree then leaned right to dodge the next one.

"Oh you won't get away that fast. You started this shit motherfucker and I'm going to finish it," Samantha said as she watched Patrick sliding down the hill on the log. She got down on one leg and raised the rifle, aimed, and squeezed the trigger. The rifle roared as a bullet came speeding out of the muzzle. The bullet slammed into Patrick's back blowing a huge hole in it. "Ahhhhhh! Dear God! Uggghhhh!" Patrick screamed in pain as the impact of the bullet knocked him forward on the log. He leaned right to change direction just as he was going to crash into a thick pine tree. "I just got to make it down the hill into town. From there, I don't care what happens to me. I just can't let that evil bitch have the satisfaction of killing me," Patrick thought to himself as he did a pull up to be able to sit up on the log right. "Uggghhhh!" he groaned in pain as blood leaked out of his back.

Samantha continued to aim using the scope on the rifle, but couldn't get a clear shot. "Fuck the bastard is moving too fast! I refuse to let him get away for killing my son," Samantha said out loud to herself, and then saw something that made her smile. She ran through the thick snow and stopped in front of the thick log and turned it straight. She strapped the hunting rifle to her back. Then she sat on the log using her body weight and feet she moved the log slowly looking like a baby in her new walker. She took big steps pushing the log until it began to slide down the snow with ease. "Oh shit! What the fuck?" Samantha screamed as she began to pick up speed, "Holy shit!" she screamed as she lost control and crashed into a tree. "Ugh ouch!" she groaned in pain while rubbing her head and shoulder. "Damn if Patrick can do it, then so can I," she said. She straightened out the log once more. "Grrrr!" the sound of growling caught her attention. She scanned the area looking left and right for any signs of movement. She heard a loud roar that caused her heart to beat fast. Samantha raised the rifle and shook the snow from her hair. "What the hell is that?" she said out loud and squinted her eyes trying her best to see through the falling snow. She could see something, but couldn't make out what it was. "What the hell is that? I just can see it's big," she said out loud to herself. Then her eyes opened wide in fear as the moving object became quite clear, as it had gotten closer and closer. At first, she swore she was seeing things and wouldn't believe it, but she was seeing it for her own eyes. A large all white Mountain Lion that looked to weigh 280 pounds was walking toward her cautiously and staring at her as if she was his next meal. The falling snow made him almost invisible, but if it wasn't for his green cat eyes that looked like a beautiful painting that mesmerized you and for the fact he had thick red blood on his fur around his mouth area.

"You gotta be fucking kidding right now!" she said in despair as the Mountain Lion charged towards her. Samantha's hand trembled and her stomach bubbled as she nervously squeezed the trigger. The bullet flew out of the gun with rapid speed. "Grrrrrrrr!" the Mountain Lion roared in pain and rage as the bullet ripped through it's left front arm. This only slowed him down for a second, and then he continued to charge towards her. Samantha saw the deranged look on the Mountain Lions face and quickly imagined what he would do to her if he got his claws into her. "Oh hell no! I don't have time to concentrate and make another shot while that thing is coming at full speed. And I'll be damned if I'm on this bitch's menu," she said out loud. She quickly hopped back on the log. She turned around to see the Mountain Lion in the air. "Ahhhhhhh! Fuck me!" she hollered knowing the Mountain Lion was about to leap on her back and tear her apart. To her surprise the log picked up speed fast. "Oweeh wooh," she said while keeping her balance and holding on for dear life.

The Mountain Lion missed her and landed on the ground. His body rolled, but pounced back up just like a cat chasing a mouse and took off running after her. "God of God," Samantha said while looking behind her at the large Mountain Lion chasing her. Then she remembered how she just crashed not too long ago. She turned her head to pay attention ahead of her leaning to the left and right. "Lord, I don't need to crash right now. God, please don't let me crash. Don't let me crash. Please don't let me crash," she mumbled over and over while leaning all her body weight to the left dodging a huge tree. She looked behind her to see the Mountain Lion running at full speed. Its paws looked as if they were barely touching the ground. "Think fast...think fast! You'll never be able to move down this mountain fast enough. He will catch up to my ass. There must be a way to outsmart him," Samantha thought to herself, then grinned as her mind formed a plan. She leaned forward making the log slide down even faster. She looked behind herself and made sure the Mountain Lion's eyes were only locked on her. "Good follow me bitch," she said out loud as she headed straight for a tree. At the last minute, she leaned right just missing the tree by inches. The Mountain Lion stumbled over his own feet trying to avoid the tree, but couldn't and slide right into the tree head first. "Hahahaha!" Samantha giggled while continuing to slide down the mountain feeling relief the Mountain Lion could no way catch up to her now. "Stupid overgrown cat!" she shouted. The thought of her husband, "It's not over yet you weak motherfucker. I'm coming for you!"

Chapter 10

A glimmer of hope sparkled in
Patrick's eyes as he could see his town Fort
Collins. He could make out the shopping
centers and hear the buses roar. Even with it
snowing so badly, people were still out
running errands and enjoying their day. The
log slid to the bottom of the mountain and
tossed him off it. He rolled three times into
the street. A blue dodge Ram pick up truck
stopped short just as the front tire was about
to roll over Patrick's head and pop it like
two fingers squeezing a grape. "Oh my God,
Patrick!" the driver of the truck shouted as
he got out. Fort Collins was home to only
thirteen hundred people making it a very
small town where everybody knew each
other and their business. The only time a
new face would pop up in the town was
hunting season to hunt mountain lions, bears,
and deer.

Patrick lied there out of breath. His
chest moved up and down as he tried to
inhale to get oxygen into his lungs. "Frank,
help me," he groaned while looking up at
the man in front of him.

Frank Mosley was 40 years old with a white beard that made him look like Santa Claus. He owned the only gas station in town and had known Patrick most of his life. "What happened Patrick? Are you okay? "Was it a hunting accident?" Frank asked with a concerned look on his face.

"No, I did this to myself. I allowed my emotions get the best of me and hurt the people I love," Patrick replied.

"You're delusional. I'm going to take you to the hospital now my old friend," Frank replied while helping him up.

Patrick groaned in pain with every move he made his body felt sore. BOOM! A shot rang Frank stopped what he was doing and looked down at his chest to see a huge hole in it. Patrick fell back to the ground. "Ahhhhhhhh!" People that were shopping on the street began to panic, screaming, and running in opposite directions that the gunfire was coming from.

Patrick laid on his back looking up at Frank who was looking down at him and the blood at the same time. Another loud shot rang out and Frank's face split open in half. He stood there twitching before falling sideways. His body made a loud thumping sound as he hit the ground and what was left of his face cracked to pieces even more like a dry eggshell being stomped on. His brain slid out of his head along with pieces of his skull. He twitched a few more times before he stopped moving altogether. "Oh shit! Holy shit!" Patrick shouted lifting his head up and could see Samantha using the log she rode down the mountain to rest to get a better aim of her target. What sent a frightening chill through Patrick's body was the fact he could see the evil smile on her face.

Samantha looked up from the scope and waved, "Don't worry you're next," Samantha said, and then quickly looked back into the rifle scope.

"Shit! Shit! Crazy woman, lord why?" Patrick said while easing himself up of the ground and did his best to run, but his body was weak. "Damn it wasn't suppose to turn out like this," he mumbled as a shot rang out and a huge hole opened up his stomach. His intestines flew to the ground and covered the snow with blood. He dropped to his knees then fell on his face losing consciousness. "Get up! Get up! Get the fuck up," he said to himself repeatedly. He slowly opened his eyes and grunted in pain. "I must keep going. I can't die like a dog," he said and began to crawl.

The smile on Samantha's face disappeared when she saw Patrick crawling. "What the fuck do I got to do to kill his ass? Why the hell won't you just die?" she screamed. Frustrated she aimed at his head then squeezed the trigger and heard a clicking sound. She squeezed the trigger once more and heard the same noise. "What the fuck," she said and cocked back the bolt of the gun to see it was emptied. "Really! Really!" she tossed the gun and looked around. She saw a lump covered in the snow and made her way over to it using her hands she removed the snow from the lump in the ground to reveal a rock. She scooped up the baseball-sized rock using both her hands and wobbled her way over to Patrick and hopped onto his back sitting on it. "Why don't you die already," she screamed at the top of her lungs while raising the rock high and coming down with full force onto the back of his head. "Ahhhhhhhhh!" Patrick screamed in agonizing pain as she raised the rock and hit once more. The blow was so hard that while Patrick was screaming with his mouth open it slammed his teeth into the pavement breaking all his front teeth. "Ahhhhhhhh!" he groaned as blood poured out of his mouth and he spit broken pieces of teeth out of his mouth.

"Die fucker die! This is for killing our son," Samantha shouted as she continued to beat the back of his head with the rock. "This is for being so soft and weak when all I needed was a real man. And you took that from me. Ahhhhhhh!" Samantha shouted as the back of Patrick's head cracked open and blood gushed and sprayed up into her mouth. "Ahhhhhhhh!" she hollered like an insane woman continuing to beat in the back of Patrick's head until it smashed in as if someone was stepping on a small mouse and its brains oozed out. "Stay dead mothefucker!" Samantha shouted knowing full well he was dead by now, but she felt as if she was in a trance and continued to pound away at what was left of the back of his head. A wicked smile spread across her face while blood was splashing everywhere on her and everywhere around.

"Freeze! Put your hands up!" the sound of a female's voice said breaking Samantha out of her trance she was in. She dropped the rock one last time on top of Patrick's body. She turned around to see Sheriff Elena pointing a gun at her. "Put your hands behind your head and don't move, Samantha," Sheriff Elena shouted and cautiously walked over to her and handcuffed her, then lead her over to the back of the police car.

"Hahahaha! It's finally over and that bastard got what he deserved. Little dick, soft love making punk," she said out loud to herself as the police car pulled off.

Chapter 11

    Sheriff Elena was Latina with brown skinned complexion and in her mid 30's. She lived in Fort Collins all of her life. She continued to glance in the rear view mirror at Samantha. "Why do you have a smile on your face, Samantha? This is a serious matter. You just killed your husband and Frank," she said.

    "Huh, I killed more than my husband. I also killed all his damn friends and no judge will convict me. Patrick duct taped me and took me to the top of the mountain with intentions on killing me. So, it was self-defense. I will get away with killing all their asses. They underestimated me and fucked with the wrong one."

    Sheriff Elena's face tightened up, "That doesn't sound like nothing Patrick would do. He was the most kindest and loved guy in town," Elena stated.

    "No, he was the softest and weakest motherfucker in town. Always trying to help someone, but not taking care of home," Samantha replied with venom in her voice.

    Elena slammed on the brakes hard causing Samantha to bump her head. Elena got out of the car and pulled Samantha out of the police car by her arm. "What the hell are you doing, Samantha?" Elena said while standing face to face. "I'm not going to keep driving and listening to this trash come out of your mouth about Patrick."

"Me killing him was self-defense. There's too much evidence. He killed my son and tried to hunt me down, but instead the roles reversed," Samantha said with a wicked grin on her face.

"Oh, so that's what you think? Because all the phone calls to the station said he was running away, then you shot him. You bashed in his skull as he crawled away."

"So what! I'll still get away with it and walk out of this God forsaken town he forced me to live in for thirteen long, damn painful years. I've despised every last one of you. Now take me to jail so I can call me a damn lawyer," Samantha said with clenched teeth.

"Everyone in town knew the only way that kindhearted man could ever snap was if he found out what everyone couldn't tell him, his best friend was having an affair with his wife. That's the only way I can only imagine Patrick losing hope finding out he lost his family. So, is that what happened bitch?" Elena replied while staring into her eyes.

"So, what if he did? He should have opened his eyes years ago and seen what was going on. Like I said, fuck you and fuck this town. Take me to jail so I can call my lawyer," Samantha couldn't finish her sentence.

Elena pulled out her gun and hit her in the head twice. "Uggghhh!" Samantha groaned as she lost consciousness and slid down the side of the car. Elena looked both ways making sure no one was around. The falling snow caused everyone to retire to their homes and no one was driving on the road. She used all her strength to drag Samantha's body to the back of the car. She opened the trunk and stuffed her in it, then closed it and hopped back into the car and drove off.

"Uggghhhh! What the fuck? Can I get a damn break today," Samantha said as her head throbbed. She opened her eyes and couldn't make out anything, but darkness feeling herself bounce up and down. "Fuck, I'm in another trunk for the day. Did that bitch really knock me out and stuff me in the trunk? I can't believe this shit," she said out loud to herself, and then felt the car come to a complete stop. She heard the car door open and Samantha began to scream like a crazy woman, "Ahhhhhhhhhhh!"

"What the fuck you screaming for? I haven't even done anything to you, yet. Besides where we are no one would hear you," Sheriff Elena said.

"Fuck you! Help! Help! Ahhhhhhhhhh!" Samantha replied and continued to scream.

"Okay, have it your way bitch," Sheriff Elena said while pulling out her 9mm from her holster and squeezed the trigger twice as a bullet slammed into Samantha's stomach and the other into the right side of her chest going through her lung. Samantha stopped screaming as she gasped for air. "I told you to stop all that damn screaming," Sheriff Elena said and grabbed Samantha's feet and pulled her out of the trunk. She flipped her on to her stomach and removed the handcuffs off of her hands.

'Relax control your breathing. Remember your military training,' she thought to herself and then scanned her surroundings. "Fuck! Fuck, not her again!" she mumbled while coughing up blood. Samantha could feel Sheriff Elena grab her legs and drag her into the woods, not too far from where the car was parked. The snow was coming down hard causing Samantha's lips to shiver. "You can't do this to me. People saw you arrest me. There's no way you can get away with it," Samantha said.

"Just watch me. The same way you're going to get away with killing Patrick. I'll get away for killing you. See what you don't know is that I served with him in Afghanistan. And he took a bullet for me. So I'll take one for him," Sheriff Elena said, then shot herself in the thigh, "Uggghhhh! That shit burns!" she said out loud, "So when I write my report, I'm going to say you took my gun and shot me," Sheriff Elena said while looking down at her.

"Your plan is stupid, bitch. They will find my body sooner or later. And they will link you to my murder, but there's just one thing I want to know. What happened in Afghanistan that made so many of you love him?" Samantha asked while giggling and coughing up blood.
Sheriff Elena stared at her before speaking, "Just know, Patrick saved a lot of us. Our unit ran across a well-known terrorist home. He killed all of the men, but discovered three million dollars in gold bars. We knew

we couldn't take the gold with the women and children as witnesses so we killed them all. Patrick was against it and tried to stop us, but it was too late. He took the lowest cut of the gold and with his share bought the house you lived in and gave his money to businesses and families in town that really needed it. The rest he was saving for Joshua. He wanted no part of what was done over there, but kept his mouth shut out of loyalty. A word I see you're not familiar with."

"Oh yea! Oh yea bitch! There will be no body of evidence for them to link me to your death," Ashanti said as she smiled sarcastically while walking out of the woods. She sat back in the police car not starting it up. She lit a cigarette and kept her eyes on Samantha.

"Uggghhhh! Stupid bitch, I swear if I make it off this mountain again I'm going to kill her slow," Samantha said, "What did she mean there would be no body for evidence? I have two bullets inside me now. That's enough to connect us," Samantha thought to herself and tried to get up, but couldn't move. Her body was too sore and blood was leaking too fast from her gunshot wounds.

Footsteps coming from the woods made her raise her head up, "Who's there?"

she said in a weak voice and couldn't see anything.

Grrrrrrrr! She heard a low growling noise and she continued to look in the direction it came from. Her heart started to beat fast as it felt as if it would stop. Only a foot away from her was the white Mountain Lion. Samantha looked at the Mountain Lion's left arm and could see where she had ripped it with a bullet. Then she looked at the Mountain Lion's face that had a sinister look masking it as if it recognized her. The Mountain Lion grinned then ran towards her and sunk her teeth into Samantha's calf muscle. "Ahhhhhhhhhhh! Fuckkkkk!" Samantha screamed in excruciating pain and was dragged into the woods.

"Like I said, there will be no body," Sheriff Elena said as she started the police car and pulled off.

Chapter 12

   The pain of the Mountain Lion's teeth deep in her flesh was too much to endure causing her to pass out. Samantha weakly opened her eyes all she could see were rocks on the ceiling and to the left of her letting her know she was in a cave. "Uggghhhh!" she moved her left hand around and found something on the right side of her. She turned her head to the right. "Nooooo! Nooooooo! Nooooooooo! Ahhhhhhhhhhh!" she screamed as tears streamed down her cheek as she stood face to face with what was left of her son. His eyes were open as if he was looking straight at her. Half of his face had been chewed off and his stomach ripped open and devoured. The meat on his arms and legs were stripped off of the bones. Samantha continued to look around in horror and could see all the bodies that were killed earlier were now in the cave picked clean of flesh and meat. Her facial expression twisted up in despair as she stared her son in the eye. "Mommy's sorry baby. Sorry," she said repeatedly and could feel water drip on her forehead. She turned her head and looked straight up to see it wasn't water, but saliva. The Mountain Lion stood over her looking down at her. "Ahhhhhhhhh!" she hollered as the Mountain Lion opened up his mouth to show its rows of razor sharp teeth. Samantha panicked knowing this was the end. "Noooo! I won't die like this," she shouted. She reached for a bone of her son's forearm and snapped it breaking it in half. The piece she now had in her hand a jagged razor sharp edge. "Ahhhhhhhh!" she let out a warrior cry and swung the sharp piece of bone in to the Mountain Loin's neck repeatedly. Grrrr! The Mountain Lion growled as blood gush out of its new wounds and fell sideways to the ground. Samantha used all her energy to hop on top of the Mountain Loin. "I won't be your dinner tonight bitch. Ahhhhhh!" Samantha screamed, then sent the sharp bone into the Mountain Lion's left side pushing it down with all her might. The Mountain Loin kicked its legs trying to buck her off, but it didn't work. His body twitched as he died. "Ha, you thought you were going to kill me. Hahaha!" Samantha said then giggled. She eased up off the Mountain Loin and weakly leaped out of the cave covered in blood and losing her own blood very fast. "Now, it's time to kill that sheriff and leave this town," Samantha said out loud.

Grrr! Grrrr! The sound of low growling made her turn around. She squinted her eyes and could see four pair of eyes leaning in closer to the Mountain Lion she had just killed. She focused and her heart raced. There were two more white Mountain Loins the same size of a human. "Oh shit!" Samantha mumbled and turned back around leaping through the woods as fast as she could.

CPSIA information can be obtained at www.ICGtesting.com
Printed in the USA
LVOW07s1018170116

471044LV00017B/576/P